THIS BOOK BELONGS TO

....

....

....

This book is dedicated to all the bears, happy and sad,
to all the children in our lives,
and to the children yet to come.
—B. S. & J. W.

SIMON & SCHUSTER BOOKS FOR YOUNG READERS
An imprint of Simon & Schuster Children's Publishing Division
1230 Avenue of the Americas, New York, New York 10020
Text copyright © 2019 by Benjamin Scheuer, Inc.
Illustrations copyright © 2019 by Jemima Williams
Music and words copyright © 2019 by Benjamin Scheuer, Inc.
All rights reserved, including the right of reproduction in whole or in part in any form.
SIMON & SCHUSTER BOOKS FOR YOUNG READERS is a trademark of Simon & Schuster, Inc.
For information about special discounts for bulk purchases, please contact Simon & Schuster Special
Sales at 1-866-506-1949 or business@simonandschuster.com.
The Simon & Schuster Speakers Bureau can bring authors to your live event.
For more information or to book an event, contact the Simon & Schuster Speakers Bureau at
1-866-248-3049 or visit our website at www.simonspeakers.com.
Book design by Lucy Ruth Cummins
The text for this book was set in 1820 Modern.
The illustrations for this book were rendered both digitally and with watercolors.
Manufactured in China
1218 SCP
First Edition
10 9 8 7 6 5 4 3 2 1
Library of Congress Cataloging-in-Publication Data
Names: Scheuer, Benjamin, author. | Williams, Jemima, illustrator.
Title: Hibernate with me / Benjamin Scheuer ; illustrated by Jemima Williams.
Description: First edition. | New York : Simon & Schuster Books for Young Readers, [2019] |
Summary: "Through the seasons, Big Bear and Small Bear share a story of love—steadfast, gentle, and
strong."— Provided by publisher.
Adapted from the song of the same name.
Identifiers: LCCN 2018001302 (print) | LCCN 2018021997 (eBook) |
ISBN 9781534432178 (hardcover) | ISBN 9781534432185 (eBook)
Subjects: | CYAC: Stories in rhyme. | Parent and child—Fiction. | Love—Fiction. | Bears—Fiction. |
Hibernation—Fiction.
Classification: LCC PZ8.3.S337 (eBook) | LCC PZ8.3.S337 Hib 2019 (print) | DDC [E]—dc23
LC record available at https://lccn.loc.gov/2018001302

HIBERNATE WITH me

WORDS BY BENJAMIN SCHEUER

PICTURES BY JEMIMA WILLIAMS

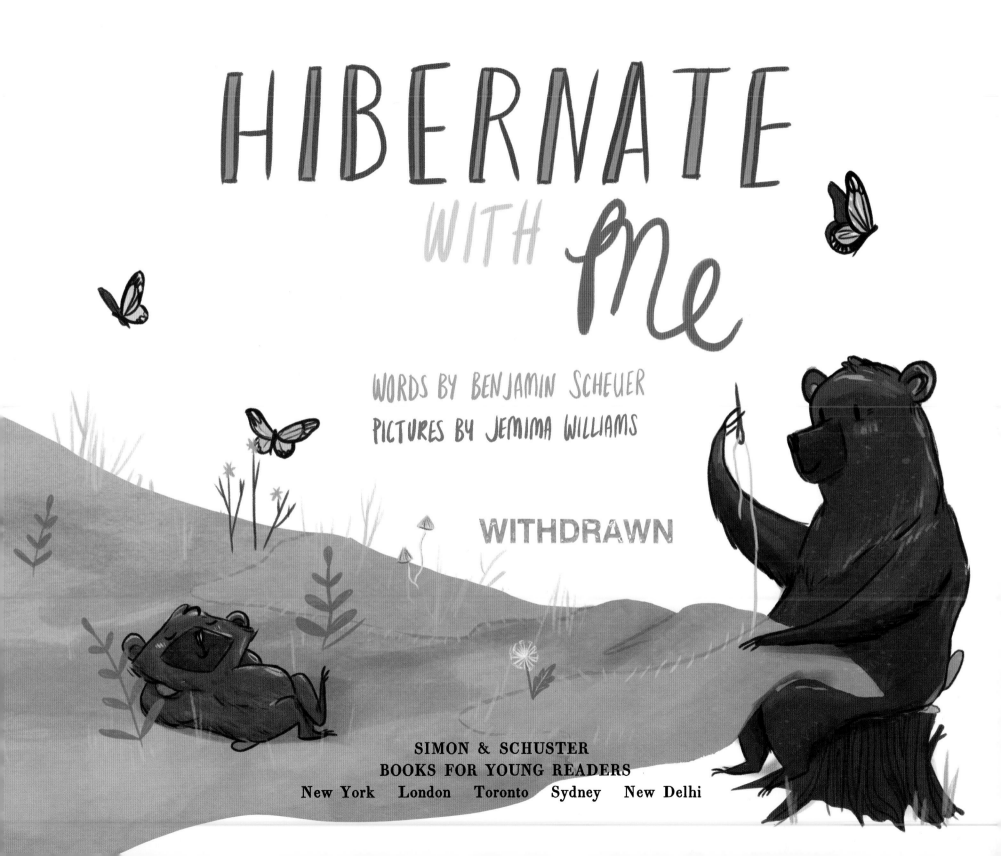

SIMON & SCHUSTER
BOOKS FOR YOUNG READERS
New York   London   Toronto   Sydney   New Delhi

Sometimes you feel small.
Sometimes you feel shy.
Sometimes you feel worried,
and you might not know why.

Sometimes you want nobody to see.

With a blanket made of meadow-moss,
I'll wrap you in a hug.

Somewhere comfortable and warm.
Somewhere cozy, safe, and snug.

I have got the perfect hollow tree.

Sometimes things can feel confusing.
Sometimes things feel gray.

But if you're ever feeling . . .

. . . lost,

I'll help you find your way.

In the autumn
when the leaves turn from green to red,

I will keep you warm.

In the winter when the wind blows cold,
you'll have a cozy bed
away from every storm.

When the spring comes
and the snow slowly melts away,
I'll be by your side.

In the summer,
we will frolic in the clover and dandelion.

But if you want to hide . . .

I'll always have a tree for you.
I'll always meet you there.

I'm always going to love you.
'Cause you're my favorite bear.

When you wake, there will be honey for your tea.

HIBERNATE WITH ME

Words and Music by
BENJAMIN SCHEUER

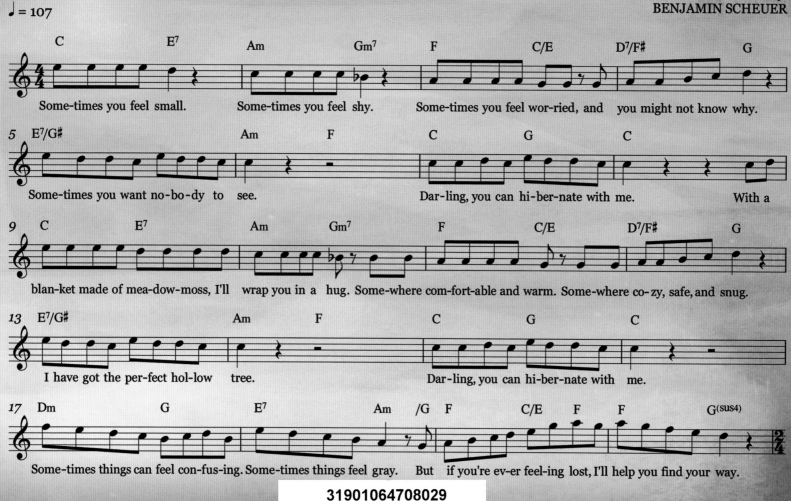